For Nicola

This edition first published in 2015 by Gecko Press
PO Box 9335, Marion Square, Wellington 6141, New Zealand
info@geckopress.com

Distributed in New Zealand by Upstart Distribution, www.upstartpress.co.nz
Distributed in Australia by Scholastic Australia, www.scholastic.com.au
Distributed in the United Kingdom by Bounce Sales & Marketing,
www.bouncemarketing.co.uk
Distributed in the United States and Canada by Lerner Publishing Group,
www.lernerbooks.com

First American edition published in 2015 by Gecko Press USA,
an imprint of Gecko Press Ltd.
A catalog record for this book is available from the US Library of Congress.

A catalogue record for this book is available from the National Library of New Zealand.

creative nz
ARTS COUNCIL OF NEW ZEALAND TOI AOTEAROA

Gecko Press acknowledges the generous support of Creative New Zealand.
Designed and art directed by Vida & Luke Kelly, New Zealand
Printed in China by Everbest Printing Co Ltd, an accredited ISO 14001
& FSC certified printer

ISBN hardback: 978-1-927271-98-8
ISBN paperback: 978-1-927271-99-5
E-book available

HELLO WORLD!

Paul Beavis

GECKO PRESS

Mr. and Mrs. Mo were busy.

They had no time to play.

"It's not fair," said the monster.

"What about me?"

"I'm sorry," said Mrs. Mo.

"We'll do something fun tomorrow."

"But I'm bored,"

grumbled the monster.

"I want to do something now,

not tomorrow."

Then he had an idea.

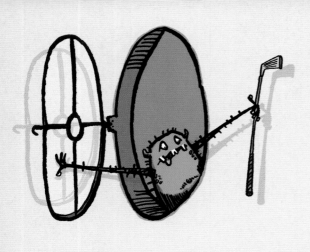

"I'm packing my bag,"
said the monster.
"I'm off to see the world."

"How exciting,"
said Mrs. Mo.
"Can I make you
a sandwich?"

"I'm okay," said the monster.

"I've got everything I need."

Soon home was far behind.

"Now this is what I call fun,"

said the monster.

A little later the monster saw a hill.

"I could climb to the top of that hill," said the monster.

"It's not far. It's just around the corner."

"Whoopee!" yelled the monster.
"Poor Mrs. Mo, missing all this fun."

And on he marched.

But after every corner, the monster found another corner.

"How much further?"
he grumbled.

"Oh dear,"
said the monster.

"I wish I'd stayed at home,"
said the monster.
"I wish I'd waited till tomorrow."

"Mrs. Mo!"
said the monster.
"You found me."

"I thought you might
be missing a few things,"
said Mrs. Mo.

"Do you have time for a sandwich?"
asked Mrs. Mo.

"Maybe just the one,"
said the monster.

Soon he felt much better.

"Come on, Mrs. Mo," he said.

"We've got a hill to climb!"

And together Mrs. Mo and the monster began to climb.

"Don't worry," said the monster. "We're nearly there."

"Hello, world!"
said the monster.

"And hello, Mr. Mo!"

"Shall we go home now?" asked Mrs. Mo.

"I can show you the way!" said the monster.

"That was fun," said Mrs. Mo.

"You're welcome,"
said the monster.
"Now, what shall
we do tomorrow?"

In the dark of winter,
Floe leapt out of the sea.

For days she hiked across the ice. It blew and it snowed. She slid and she stumbled, but she never once stopped to rest.

Sometimes she tobogganed; often she had to climb.

She was on her way to meet her mate Fin.

Just as the struggle began to seem endless,
Floe's heart quickened. She could hear a
great noise in the distance.

Up ahead, the horizon was dark with
penguins as they gathered in their thousands.
The colony grew and grew as more arrived
each minute. She was nearly home.

Floe bustled through the rookery, calling for Fin. If he'd survived the months at sea, he would be out there somewhere looking for her too.

For hours she called. Then, far away in the forest of noise, she thought she heard him. She called, then listened. Faintly, his voice echoed back. It was Fin!

Floe called again. Fin replied. She followed the sound she knew so well.

And there he was at last. They bowed and stretched with delight. They touched chests. Fin led Floe on a celebration walk. They were together again.

A few weeks later, their voices sang out
with pride. Floe had laid her egg.
She passed it to Fin. He took it
onto his feet, gently covered
it from the cold and
prepared for the
long, hungry
wait.

Again they sang and then Floe was gone – on the
big journey back to the sea to collect food for
the baby.

At the water's edge she hesitated. She was
desperate to swim, but something made her stop.

Then she saw it…

…a leopard seal! Just beneath the ice, ready to snatch her as she dived in. Floe stood still and waited.

Eventually, the seal flicked the surface and set off, looking for less careful penguins to hunt.

Floe splashed into the clear water and twisted down into the deep.

Back in the rookery, Fin huddled with the other penguins to keep warm.

For three bitter months, he had been without food and still he protected the egg.

Then, one morning, he heard a tapping sound. Slowly, the egg began to crack. Fin watched in wonder as the shell broke open and the baby was born. The first thing baby Solo saw was a winter storm.

Floe wasn't back from the sea, so Fin fed her what little oil he had.

Excitement grew as the first fat females returned. All around them, other chicks were starting to hatch.

At last Floe arrived. The sight of Fin with baby Solo filled her with joy. She bowed and bumped against Fin. He passed her the baby. They showed cheeks and sang, and Solo got her first good meal of squid.

Then, desperate with hunger,
Fin set straight off for the sea.
It was his turn to collect
the food.
    He splashed with delight.
He tumbled and swam. For weeks
he dived and fished.

At the rookery, Solo was growing well.
Floe had run out of food, but Fin was
a good diver. He'd soon be back with
plenty of squid. Then she could go
fishing again.

One morning, Floe and Solo saw
dark shapes approaching in the
distance – fat, waddling penguins!
They could hardly wait.

But Fin wasn't among the first
ones back. They could only watch as
all around them chicks were fed
and hungry mothers were finally free to
go to sea.

Each time more penguins arrived, their spirits rose. But still Fin didn't come.

Days passed. Anxiously, they watched as the last few stragglers came home. Perhaps Fin had got lost? Or perhaps he'd gone farther than the others to find good food?

Solo cried with hunger, but Floe had nothing left to feed her. She was hungry too. And now there were no more shapes in the distance to give them hope.

Floe waited one more day. And when Fin didn't come, she knew she would have to leave her chick or they would both starve. She put Solo on the snow, looked back once, then hurried off towards the sea. It was a faint hope, but perhaps she could make the trip in time to save her chick.

Solo tried to follow, but she couldn't keep up. She waited quietly for a while, but then she cried out from the cold.

A few heads turned. Some of the penguins noticed that Solo was on her own.

One penguin tried to drag her onto his feet, but another pulled her from behind. A third tugged at her flipper. Suddenly, five large penguins were fighting over Solo. They all wanted to care for her, but they tugged and nipped so hard that she cried out with fright.

Scurrying away, Solo slid
down a crevice. At the
bottom she lay awhile,
panting with shock. Curious
faces peered down at her.
At least she was safe
from their jabbing beaks.

Slowly she recovered, and soon had the strength
to struggle along the bottom. At one end, the space
opened up and Solo found herself at the edge of the
rookery. From there, she set off to find her mother.

She hadn't gone far when a skua bird swooped down, knocking Solo to the ground. She cried and tumbled; then a gust of wind blew her down again, bowling her over and over. The wind blew harder. She rolled and slid along the ice.

The skua fought the wind, waiting to dive again.

Solo called for her mother but she was far away, still hurrying to the sea. She struggled to her feet and looked back. The rookery was out of sight.

A bitter wind bowled her over again. And this time she
didn't get up. She lay on the ice, weak and shivering.
   The skua landed and settled its wings, ready
for an easy meal. It reached forward, nipped at
Solo's belly and began to tug.
   Solo cried out...

...and a passing shape stopped. It hobbled over and lunged at the skua.

Fin was back!

He had finally managed the journey, dragging the fisherman's net the whole way with him.

Weeks later, to Fin and Solo's delight, they heard a familiar sound across the icy wastes – a half-hearted call from Floe.

At once they both replied. And for a wonderful moment they listened to Floe getting closer, calling with joy and disbelief.